THING OF DARKNESS

Positronic Publishing
PO Box 632
Floyd VA 24091

ISBN 13: 978-1-62755-086-4

First Positronic Publishing Edition
10 9 8 7 6 5 4 3 2 1

THING OF
DARKNESS

G. G. PENDARVES

I

A long curving sweep of tall gray houses. At their feet the old parade, its worn seawall banked up against wind-driven tides. Troon House, grayer, gaunter than the rest, stood empty. A signboard creaked on rusted hinges, advertising it For Sale or To Let.

Lonely. Lovely. Deserted. Seagate was proud of Troon House. Seagate was afraid of it. People came by the score to see it, always in broad daylight. They were careful to keep in groups, silent, timid, turning a sharp corner, entering each unexplored room with that sudden jolt that a clumsily manipulated elevator gives to one's heart.

They stared at beautiful restorations, at blackened beams, at vast wall-cupboards, and at brick fireplaces whose ancient clay showed every tint of umber, rose and purple-brown. They bunched together closely going up the last steep narrow stairs to the west attic. They looked at its deep recess, recently and fatally uncovered—looked and shuddered.

They went in close order downstairs again, escaped through low-roofed, retiled kitchens to a long untended garden behind the house and thence to a broad lane and main road at last. Shaken, nervously loquacious, they didn't speak of Troon until the old place was out of sight. Over tea and famous Seagate shrimps they exchanged impressions.

Going home after sunset, if they stayed so long, they glanced in passing along the road, at Troon's blank front windows, shivered, looked quickly away.

Troon—gray old house, left to hideous memories of the Thing of Darkness. Day by day, night by night, through the years, through the centuries Troon had stood. Old, forsaken, betrayed. Old Troon—shell of death—old Troon.

Low sullen clouds. A cold northwest wind. Fierce squalling gusts of rain. A high angry tide, gray-green flecked with bitter white, roaring up the estuary. Seagate was a mile of wet gray road and blank-faced houses. Wind and sea . . . wind and sea.

At the village-church of Keston, a fifteen minute walk away on the hill behind, the broken body of Joe Dawlish with its staring tortured eyes and twisted face of fear was being buried. And in another grave, a sad small grave, the bones of "Lizzy Werne were being laid to rest after three hundred years delay.

People thronged the small churchyard to its broad low moss-stained walls. From Seagate, from Keston, from all over the Wirral peninsula, and even from Liverpool and Chester they had come to witness this double funeral. Reporters, psychic investigators, university professors rubbed wet shoulders with fishermen, farmers, shop-keepers and local gentry.

At the end, the very end when the last words of the service were said and it only remained for the gaping graves to be filled in, the vicar stood with uplifted hands.

His somber gaze looked out over the crowd to tossing trees and lowering sky. His lined face, wet with rain, was worn and anxious.

*

Suddenly his voice rang out again, a cry from the heart of this shepherd of a stricken flock . . . "Deliver us, O Lord, from all assaults of the devil! In thine infinite mercy, protect and succor us! Stretch forth thy hand against this Thing of Darkness and set us free from fear! In the name of Him who died for us—Amen."

There was a murmurous response like water breaking on a distant shore. Then, slowly, silently, pelted by spiteful icy rain, the crowd dispersed.

At the lich-gate Doctor Dick Thornton was pushed up against two people he wanted to avoid: Edith and Alec Kinloch. Alec's heavy sallow face showed distinct traces of emotion. He looked quite appealingly at Doctor Dick.

"'Fraid I didn't take all this quite seriously before," he confessed. "I don't understand what it's all about, but—"

Edith put a restraining hand on his arm. He was having one of his emotional moments, she could see. Heaven knew what he might say! Probably he would double his already absurdly generous offer of five pounds to the widow. What a blessing she could count on herself never to lose her head! Queer sort of service it had been. These villagers adored emotional orgies. Well, poor things, they must have some pleasure in their dull stupid lives. Clever of the vicar to stage such a good show for them. He knew how to cater for a rural diocese.

To deflect her husband from possible weakness she turned to the young girl behind her.

"Lynneth, this is Doctor Thornton. He's a sort of uncle to all the fishermen of Seagate. Miss Lynneth Brey, Doctor Thornton. A connection of my husband's. She's going to spend a month or so with us—at Troon."

There, Edith thought, that'll let him know right off that they've not succeeded in scaring us. Her tactics were wasted. The doctor didn't even hear her. He was looking down into Lynneth's uplifted rosy face. Black eyes, soft, sooty, heart-catching. Eyes made for tears and laughter and—oh, yes! he knew at once— made for love. He looked deep, deeper into them; young, radiant, kindled with recent deep emotion. Eyes to light a man's path, to draw him on and up, above life's dusty sordid clamor. Eyes that promised and withheld.

Doctor Dick's feet were treading air, his heart thumped with the beat-beat-beat of hooves on a hollow road, his head felt full of fizzy champagne. But no one guessed it. He heard his voice, it didn't seem to surprise anyone, replying to the introduction. He waited with parted lips, eyes a clear tender blue, listening—listening for her voice.

"Oh!" She considered him. A smile drew her lips in an adorable sideways quirk. "You make me feel homesick, although I've only been here a day. You speak like a Highlander."

"I am one. From Gairloch."

She put out a small hand to be enveloped in his close grip, and laughed in quick delight.

"That's my place. My own darling funny village. My mother's birthplace. We've got a cottage there. D'you remember it— the one like a brown loaf at the head of Glen Ruach?"

*

They drifted from the church-gate, away down the twisting road. The crowd of people might have been blown wet leaves. The two Kinlochs, left behind, exchanged long glances.

"Let 'em go." Alec took his wife's arm. "Birds of a feather—eh? She and Pills can keep each other amused. Looks like a case to me. You won't be bothered with her long."

"Really, Alec! There's the garage—what on earth are you dragging me on for? I'm certainly not going to hang about for that silly girl. Going off with a man she's just met, like that! She behaves like a child. No idea of appearances."

"What odds? Nobody's going to notice a kid like that."

"Nonsense! She's connected with us. D'you want him for a permanent relation?"

"Why not? Get the girl off your hands while the going's good. She and Pills would run a dispensary or a nursing-home and be too busy to interfere with us. This yearly visit's beginning to pall."

She glanced shrewdly at him. "Something in that. And even if he's queer, quite important people have taken him up. Come on, then. I'm perishing with cold. This sensed fuss! Seagate doesn't seem to have altered since Troon House was first built."

They clambered into their car and splashed down the lane to their bungalow by the marshes.

*

"Quite! Quite! However, there are always two sides to everything."

Mr. Alec Kinloch presented a large bulwark of flesh from behind which his schoolboy's mind issued bulletins to the outside world. He kept a store of such ready-made bulletins within, stereotyped responses calculated to give intimation of a subtle discerning intellect at work. He would employ such tactics indefinitely if conducting a conversation unaided. If his wife was with him she manned the big guns while he posed as an impregnable fortress.

Doctor Dick regarded the large dull pretentious creature with patience born of his profession rather than his temperament. Doctor Dick was a Highlander. Alec Kinloch a Lowland Scot. This, in itself, was a deep fixed gulf between them, apart from gulfs of breeding and intellect, and today the doctor found his host peculiarly trying. He'd made a point of calling when he knew Lynneth would not be at Sandilands. He wanted to spare her the grim tale he had to tell. It had been an effort, however; to miss a chance of seeing her, and his mood grew steadily darker.

"What," he demanded, "would you consider the other side of this horror at Troon?"

Baffled at such direct attack, Alec poked at his pipe with an air of grave reserve. He and Edith always were careful to be non-committal in their attitude until they discovered the trend of popular feeling with reference to a new idea. This Troon ghost notion now! If Seagate took it seriously, and yesterday's funeral service seemed to indicate so, then they would follow suit. Alec had been swayed by the vicar yesterday. Now, however, he knew Edith's view was the really intelligent and logical one. The vicar had been simply playing up, doing what the villagers expected of him. Jolly good thing no one but his wife knew that he'd actually got the wind up yesterday. The "Thing of Darkness!" Uh! Nasty phrase that! He'd felt like chucking up everything—selling Troon to any fool who wanted the old place. Well, he could laugh at himself and his fears now.

But this young Pills! He seemed officious. Trying to interfere. Pulling all this stuff about haunts and devils at Troon. Warning him that the workmen restoring the old house were in danger and that he and Edith ought to give up all idea of living there. Damned young whippersnapper, sitting there at his ease and telling a man of the world what was what! He'd tell him where he got off all right!

The door opened to admit his wife. Alec crossed his legs, resumed his pipe, took up the fortress-pose as Doctor Dick rose to his feet. Edith Kinloch progressed with ceremony to a chair.

"How nice of you to call again —so soon, Doctor Thornton."

"Doctor Dick" corrected the visitor. "My father is still in practise here. We have to make a distinction."

"Oh! How awkward for you!"

Edith was slim and tall and neat. She was invariably bright and kind too. It was part of her chosen role to stoop kindly to her inferiors. The Lady Bountiful was her favorite part, to be gracious, to condescend. She'd been these things infuriatingly and increasingly ever since she cut free from her decent but quite uneducated family at the age of fourteen. Alec never knew to this day that her mother had a fish-and-chips shop in Edgware road, that her father was crippled and on the dole, that her younger sisters were working in a glue factory.

"My wife," Alec would tell you, believing it to be a fact, "lost both her parents—died in India when she was a child. Friends made themselves responsible for her education" (the Local Educational Council as represented by Edith's adaptable mind) "a branch of the Dorsetshire Frome-Stoddarts, you know. Good old family but impoverished—impoverished."

Edith smiled brightly on the two men sitting before the study fire.

"I'm sure you must be cold and hungry, Doctor—Dick, if you insist on the familiarity. I just went to tell cook she must drop everything and make some of her famous hot cakes for tea. Cook is so difficult, but really I find the best thing is to alter her routine every now and then. I do it on principle."

She proceeded to stage-manage a background for an afternoon-tea act. Doctor Dick was used as scene-shifter. Edith directed him with firm smiling competence. He pulled up tables and pushed away chairs. She conveyed atmospherically that he was young and insignificant enough to do these things rather than Alec.

And now do let's go on with all that too adorable tale you were telling us about Troon just now. So like a story of Edgar Allan Poe's. Now don't say you finished that tale while I was out of the room! No? That's right!"

She beamed approval.

"Now. We're all settled. Tea—and put on another log, Alec, the basket's beside you there—a real Christmas fire to warm you up, Doctor Dick. And eat up the scones; you must be needing something. No use calling at tea-time and not taking advantage of the fact."

Glittering gracious hostess. Her varnished toffee-brown eyes shone in the firelight. She addressed the doctor as if he were a schoolboy out for a treat. She was convinced he'd arranged purposely to call at their tea hour. So lean and hungry-looking! She plumed herself on the observation! She plumed herself on the observation which thus misread Doctor Dick's rigidly disciplined muscular body.

"This is the only time I can call," the doctor was young enough to feel not amused at her patronage. "I pass this bungalow on my way up to Keston. Due at the hospital at five, you know." Edith smiled her best worldly understanding smile. Let the young man get away with his excuses, poor dear. She didn't grudge him his tea. Pity Lynneth was out. It would have been easy then to sidetrack him from the mission he felt he had concerning Troon and its restoration. She must make things plain, perfectly plain, once and for all. She leaned forward. Her glistening eyes, her perfectly smooth face, her small ungenerous mouth registered smiling cordiality.

"Now do tell me all about it."

*

Doctor Dick's blue eyes grew black and gray as the November afternoon. He told her. Told her details of Joe Dawlish's death. Told her of daily increasing peril at Troon. Implored her to give up the whole thing, to leave the gray haunted old house to its evil.

"The men are in hourly danger—horrible danger. You are letting loose forces that have been pent up in the place for centuries. The men should come off the job at once."

At his increasingly urgent manner, Alec and Edith Kinloch stiffened simultaneously. After all, dash it all, the house is mine, ran Alec's thoughts, and there's a limit to the interference one can stand! Edith's eyes answered his unspoken protest, agreeing with it.

Alec voiced his ideas. His tone was a subtle reproach.

"Was this Joe Dawlish working on the house when he died?"

"He was." The doctor's clipped reply roused all Alec's fathomless obstinacy.

"I suppose he was insured."

Alec's own instant perception of the vital core of this queer fuss about Dawlish gratified him enormously. He was moved, without waiting for his wife's lead, to make a gesture.

"Well, I might give the wife a little extra. Ten pounds would pay for the funeral—handsomely. These people love a ghoulish sort of feast, don't they? 'Buried him with ham'—what!"

"Ham? Er, yes . . . quite. Ham."

Doctor Dick looked his host up and down as if he saw some connection between him and the word he reiterated. He got to his feet.

He was out of the room, out of the little entrance-hall, out of the house—stalking like a long- legged bird down the garden and on to the road almost before Edith and Alec could reply to his swift farewell. He'd been so quick, so cumbered with hat, stick and a knobby untidy parcel, that he didn't even shake hands.

*

Alec threw himself down in his armchair by the fire, took up a brass toasting fork and began to warm up the remaining scones. Edith watched him absent-mindedly.

"Shut Pills up, didn't I?" he spoke with his mouth full of scone. "Nothing like getting down to brass tacks with these fellows. Driveling about spooks and Troon! Neat dodge for collecting for Dawlish's widow. Better do the thing handsomely, as we're strangers here. Living at the big house, we'll be obliged to play up a bit."

Edith continued her pursuit of abstract thought.

"Well?"

"Yes, dear."

She came out of her trance, sat forward inelegantly, a thin hand on either knee. Strong emotion did occasionally uncover the past.

"Alec, there's more in this than meets the eye. Mark my words, there's someone else after Troon. They want to turn us out, force us to sell. I dare say they've found how old and much more valuable the property is than they believed. Let 'em try!"

He wolfed the last scone, pulled out a large white linen handkerchief, polished his lips, arranged his mustache, hitched up his trousers at the knee and lighted a fresh pipe.

"Let 'em!" he echoed in profound sepulchral tones.

*

Six o'clock on a late November evening. Rain and a squalling wind from the east. A high tide slapping and hissing against the mile-long ancient seawall.

Jim Sanderson drove at his job in the cold drafty house with nervous hurry. A highly intelligent able workman was Jim, the best workman of the gang at Troon House.

Well over three hundred years old the house was. Of late it had fallen into bad disrepair. Its landlord lived in Ireland and had rented his fine old derelict to one careless tenant after another until roof and walls let in as much weather as they kept out.

The Liverpool agent happened to love the house. He had done his best, wrested small sums from its owner for patching here and patching there for forty odd years. But he and Troon could bluff no longer.

Would-be tenants kept on coming, for a genuine old Seagate house for sale was rare. Their verdict was unanimous. Damp! Rain drove in through deep cracks and faulty windows. Salt water used in the cement made ugly discolorations everywhere. Timbers were rotting. One roof had curvature of the spine. Toads and spiders had taken over ruined outbuildings and kitchens. Weeds, coarse grass, overgrown hedges and dumps of rubbish made a desert of the long garden at Troon's back.

At last, the agent had put up enormous startling bills in each of Troon's front windows. And, suddenly, he sold the house.

The two Kinlochs had seen it. They had money. They needed an old and mellow background. They got a first-class architect to vet the place, found a reasonable sum would make it weatherproof, beat the Irish landlord down a little—very little, for he was savage as a cornered rat. Followed a flurry of contracts, plans, and agreements, then parleyings with the local council, who mistrusted haste and people with money to spend on a damp derelict house in Seagate. And the Kinlochs were in a hurry: they wanted to settle in before Christmas.

At last Troon House legally changed hands. The Kinlochs rented a bungalow lurking a mile away by the marshes. Troon was delivered up to the builders and decorators.

And so we return to Jim Sanderson on this gloomy November evening.

*

He had an electric torch, for no light was yet installed in the house. By its beam he prodded furiously at a patch of decayed timber by the hearthstone. A specimen was demanded by the Mycology Section of the Forest Products Research Laboratory. Dry rot was suspected in this large front room on the ground floor. Sanderson had to send his specimen by that night's post. The other workmen were gone. He was working overtime—alone.

Clap! Clap! Clap!

Somewhere in the drafty darkness upstairs a door banged persistently. It got on his nerves. He was a sensitive man in spite of his big muscular frame. Temperament, imagination, nerves were part of his quick flexible intelligence. He hated this night job. He felt queer and jumpy.

Clap! Clap! Clap!

There! The damned door had shut itself at last. He heaved a sigh of relief. Then his scalp prickled. Was someone up there? Had they shut the door? Was that someone coming down the broken creaking staircase?

The whites of his eyes showed like those of a frightened horse as he glanced up at the rain- blurred glass of a large bay-window on his right. Impulse seized him to dash himself at the panes, to escape to the friendly old parade just outside. Overwhelmingly he wanted to be out in the open—to exchange this dusty musty shelter for rain and salt wind and flying scuds of foam.

He'd had enough. Things had got worse ever since Joe Dawlish had pulled down the cupboard in the big west attic a week ago. The wall and chimney-breast had crumbled and broken with its removal. A few stout blows, and the whole false facade had come down, revealing a deep recess reaching from rafters halfway to floor. On the broad stone shelf thus formed, a skeleton lay.

The bones of a child. Skull smashed in. A staple and chain padlocked round the bone of the left arm. The padlock was the strangest thing of all, of black smooth heavy stone with queer red markings chalked on it.

The vicar had been summoned in a hurry. He'd brought Doctor Dick with him. They were in a great taking about the affair, and carried off the poor little bones for burial.

From that hour things had gone wrong at Troon. Joe, who'd found the bones, was dead and buried inside a week—and what a week, too!

*

Sanderson's big brown hands fumbled as he tugged and strained at the flooring. He felt suddenly hot and weak. There was a flurry in his brain. He wrenched out the piece of wood he needed, stowed it roughly away in a torn capacious pocket of his old coat. Still on his knees, he gathered up his tools.

He rattled and banged things about, trying to shut out other sounds . . . sounds on the stairs . . .

The breath seemed to stop in his big body.

Creak. Creak. Creak.

It was someone cautiously stealing downstairs.

Crack!

He knew that sound. It was broken step, third from the bottom. He tried to call out. It must be that damned oaf, Walter! The fool must have gone to sleep up there. Sanderson couldn't make his stiff dry tongue obey him. He couldn't hail whoever it was out there. He couldn't—he daren't.

His hunted eyes sought the window. Power to move, to jump for it, had left him. He knelt there, powerful shoulders hunched, hands on the floor for support, crouched like a big frightened animal. He fought to prevent himself looking over his shoulder at the door behind. He knew it was opening. He heard stealthy fingers on the old loose knob. He heard the harsh scrape of wood on wood as the sagging door was pushed back.

Ice-cold wind blew in, rustled bits of paper and shavings on the floor.

Sanderson's head jerked back to look. The door stood widely open. His eyes, filmed with terror, focused achingly on the gap between door and wall. Darkness moved there. A Thing Of Darkness. On the threshold it bulked in shapeless moving menace. Darkness made visible . . . blotting out everything . . . blotting out life itself.

The crash of a small wooden crate on which his heavy hand rested saved Sanderson from fainting. He leaped for the window. Glass cracked and fell in sharp tinkling showers. A thick cloth cap protected his lowered head. He was through. He fell on the strip of trampled grass outside, among a tangle of ladders and buckets. He vaulted the pointed iron railing and was in the road—running—running— breath coming in deep sobbing gusts—deathly face splashed with rain and blood.

Ahead shone the cheerful red and white lamp of the Three Mariners. He went straight for it as a fox for a familiar burrow.

Mr. and Mrs. Burden—old Tom and old Mary to most—who kept the Three Mariners were sitting in their vast red-tiled kitchen before a blazing fire. Black hand-made rugs were spread. Oil lamps of heavy brass hung from massive black oak rafters. At a round walnut table covered with a crimson cloth, Mrs. Burden was working placidly through a pile of stockings to be mended. Solomon, a great tawny Persian cat, dozed with its leonine head on her instep. Mr. Burden, smoking a long churchwarden, sat in a wide Windsor chair glossy with age and use, his stockinged feet on a gleaming wrought-brass stool.

Doctor Dick sprawled on a settle nearby. Two or three fishermen, warming up before the tide turned and they put out for their night's catch, completed the little company of friends.

They all looked up at the loud bang of the outer door. Every face was turned toward the kitchen entrance when Jim Sanderson burst in.

"For God's sake—a drink!"

He collapsed into a big chair and sat with head down on his hands, shivering and gasping before the hot fire. Doctor Dick was at his side in a moment. Mrs. Burden ran for a drink. Mr. Burden dropped his favorite pipe and stared. The fishermen sat forward, hands on knees, consternation on their weathered red-brown faces. Solomon stood with arched back, great feathery tail waving nervously, before seeking shelter under a distant chair to await developments.

Sanderson told his experience in jerks between sips of the Three Mariners' best Jamaica rum. His audience blinked, muttered, stared. Doctor Dick, that brilliant modern young man, listened with flattering and tremendous concentration, sea-blue eyes and keen face losing every trace of their habitual friendly good-humor.

Mrs. Burden sat immobile. She had, as always, a flavor of the wild, of a remote and more instinctive age, of ancient beliefs and wisdom. She moved like a feather in a draft of wind—so light, so frail, so incalculable. She always seemed curiously unrelated to furniture and rooms and human dwelling-places in spite of making the Three Mariners the coziest inn in the whole county of Cheshire. She had the quality of some dear deep peat-brown river, nourishing the earth and nourished by it.

Her husband, rocklike as she was fluid and quick, turned to her now.

"What d'yer say to that, old woman? That there Troon house was always what you might say queer-like. I reckon it's had queer folk in it and all. But I never heard tell of anything out and out bad."

"No? Well, I did, then."

Doctor Dick leaned forward, pipe in hand, his eyes bright as blue steel in the lamp-glow.

"Now this isn't treating me on the level, old Mary." He waved his pipe in reproach. "You know very well the vicar and I are trying to rake up Troon's past history. I've been here for the last hour and you've never let out one solitary squeak."

"No, and I wouldn't have done it if Jim hadn't seen what he has seen this night." Her bright dark eyes flashed round the intent faces.

"I've been thinking over that business you've been telling about, Doctor Dick, that skeleton Joe dug out of the walls last week. Seems like as if that must have been her skeleton."

No one contradicted this dark surmise.

"I'll tell you the story as my grandfeyther's grandfeyther wrote it. He was a scholar. Kept village school up at Keston. He'd got an old book with everything put down that happened since Seagate began. I read this story when I was a girl and never forgot a word. I can get the book from my uncle's niece by marriage that works in a big library up to London to prove I'm right."

*

Chairs were hitched up, pipes relit. Old Tom flung a log that roused the fire to crackling flame. Solomon emerged, paced majestically back to his mistress, stretched at her feet with his yellow chin supported on them.

"The year 1600 saw Troon put up at the end of the parade, only a low seawall then. Course Troon was naught but a little tavern then: Troon Tavern. Even for those rough times it was a bad place. They had miners over from Flint across the water—dark little devils, those Welshmen, always scrapping and more handy with knives than a butcher himself. Mostly it was miners went to Troon Tavern. The man that built it was Thomas Werne, a Seagate man that got hold of money somehow. Smuggling, most like.

"Werne, the book said, was nothing but a block brute of a man. Treated his young wife wors'n dog. When she died he got downright savage, and the child, Lizzy, left to him, came in for it all. I'm not going to harrow your feelings nor my own by telling what that innocent suffered. Laws weren't much then when it came to looking after poor people's children.

"But there was a gentleman came to stay here at this very inn, the Three Mariners, and he was that angry when he saw Lizzy and learned about her from Seagate talk, he threatened he'd have Werne put in prison. The gentleman went back to London after that and told Werne he'd hear more about it. Well, next thing that happened was—Lizzy Werne disappeared."

"Ah!" Doctor Dick's voice poignantly expressed his thought.

"Yes. Everyone was certain sure Werne had done it, same as you're thinking yourself," responded old Mary. "But nothing could be proved. The body of the child, not much more of it than bones Joe found, never turned up, search though they might and did! The law made a great fuss when it was too late. The gentleman from London came back and he stayed for weeks, he was that set on getting Werne hanged for murder."

"And he walled the child up in his own house, then!" Doctor Dick's eyes blazed.

"Aye. After three hundred years we've found what Werne did, I b'lieve!"

"Eh, think of that!" Old Tom spat into the red fire. "And what did the murderin' fellow say had happened to the child? What did he tell 'em?"

"Said she was drowned. No one ever knew whether or not she was, the tides being mortal quick and dangerous here at Seagate. An' 'twas worse then. There were quicksands down by the marshes, and more than Werne's Lizzy had been caught and drowned. No one believed Werne's tale, only nothing could be done to him because Lizzy's body was never found."

"Quite. What I don't see," put in Doctor Dick, "is why he walled the body up. After smashing her skull, why not have taken the corpse out to sea and dropped it overboard one dark night?"

Old Mary shook her head.

"You mean he hadn't a boat?"

"No, I don't mean that, Doctor Dick. All the Seagate men had boats in those days, same as you and me have a pair of shoes. Reckon you're the only one here doesn't know why he couldn't put that body in the sea."

There were confirmatory nods all-round the silent spellbound circle. Doctor Dick frowned in bewilderment.

"Why?"

"Well, seeing you don't know, I'll say the verse that was in the old book my grandfeyther's grandfeyther wrote out;

> "A murdered body cast to sea
> May never there lie quietly,
> But every night is washed ashore,
> And standing by the murderer's door
> It cries to be let in.

"Of course that's put in rhyme and it's not quite right about the tides, not being a high tide every night anyhow. But the tide or no tide, the ghost would come back to the man who did the murder every night of his life."

Jim Sanderson shivered and looked with haunted eyes at the old woman.

"You reckon I saw her then—the ghost?"

"No. There's one, and it's a downright dangerous one. The child escaped, thanks be! But Werne's caught himself now and he's going to make people suffer for it."

She turned to Doctor Dick.

"That padlock you told me about, with the red marks on it. Magic that was, black magic to keep the child's soul a prisoner all these years. Sold her to the devil, did her father! Just so long as the child was promised. Werne himself was free." Sanderson made an abrupt movement.

"I don't know as I get your meaning, old Mary."

"Plain enough. He'd sold his child to the devil, same as you'd bind an apprentice. The devil, he taught Werne how to lock her up safe so as her little ghost couldn't escape and go wandering round, making people suspect. Well, that spell was broker when Joe Dawlish broke down the wall and the padlock and chain."

"As far as that goes," Doctor Dick's crisp voice interrupted the old woman's uncomfortably clear exposition, "the vicar and I are equally to blame."

"And Werne's not going to forget it," warned old Mary. "Now Lizzie's bones lie in the churchyard all safe and sound there'll be trouble—black trouble. That's how I see it, anyways."

Jim sucked in his breath on a long tremulous hiss. The fishermen got to their feet.

"Reckon the tide's right enough now," said one.

"Wait! I'll come along." Jim lunged clumsily in the wake of the retreating men. "You're going my road and I'll be glad of company tonight."

Old Mary's serious withdrawn look followed the group out. As the heavy outer door banged to, she shook her head.

"Jim Sanderson's in for it," she said in a low voice. "After sunset it's asking for trouble to set foot in Troon. He'll go like Joe Dawlish went. Poor fellow . . . poor fellow!"

*

The next afternoon, Troon stood in a blaze of sunlight. The sky was mother-of-pearl. A slow full tide gleamed like gray satin. Troon confronted it—cold, indifferent, implacable.

Inside its strong walls an army of workmen went about like busy scurrying ants. They were desperate to finish this job. Work that would ordinarily have lingered on for weeks was being rushed through at treble speed. One week more would see painting and decorations complete. Even the long wilderness of a garden was being dug and planted and trimmed and sown at a pace contrary to all Seagate tradition.

Doctor Dick lingered outside the strip of grass and iron rail protecting Troon's tall front windows on the ground floor. Lynneth had told him she was coming with the Kinlochs about three o'clock this afternoon. Elaborate juggling with his day's appointments brought him to Troon on the stroke of the hour.

"Afternoon, doctor!"

A joiner called Frost touched his cap. He carried a big woven basket of tools over his shoulder. His face looked bleached. He glanced back over his shoulder as he stepped from Troon's front door and blinked in the clear light outside the house.

"Knocking off already?"

"Aye, sir. Not worth going to fetch more tools for half an hour."

Doctor Dick stared. Laughed. "You don't mean your day finishes at three-thirty, Frost? I envy you."

"There's none of us works there," he jerked a backward thumb, "after three-thirty, sir. Not these short days. All on us goes at three-thirty—before dusk," he added with significance.

"I see. How do you square that up with regulations?"

"We begins at seven 'stead of eight o' mornings, sir. That's how we does it. The boss is agreeable so long as we does a regular day all told."

"Leave before sundown. Yes, I see."

"We've got good reasons for it."

"I believe you."

"Aye. Not a man would stay in Troon after dusk. No—not for a ransom, not since Jim Sanderson went. A cruel death! Went like Joe Dawlish—just the same."

Seeing the doctor's grave expression, Frost began speaking again.

"Mark my words, sir, if them two iggerant foreigners—if you'll excuse me putting it so bald-like —wot are renting the bungalow over by the marshes—"

"Mr. and Mrs. Kinloch?"

"Aye. If them two move into Troon next week, all I say is they'd do better to go down marsh-walk and be drowned comfortable. Might as well die natural deaths like! That's wot I says and wot I sticks to."

Doctor Dick took this with gratifying seriousness. He went to his car and fiddled about with it for a minute or so to gain time, then returned with a thought he appeared to have found under the car's hood.

"Look here, Frost! Believing in anything makes it real. If the Kinlochs have no faith at all in old Werne and his power to hurt them, well, perhaps he cannot."

Frost poked his head forward like a turtle emerging from its shell.

"Noa," his north-country accent marked strong emotion, "I doan't hold wi' thot and thee doesn't neether, Doctor Dick! Thot oogly Thing a-grinnin' and a-murderin' there in the dark like, it's naught to it what we b'lieves! It just bides quiet—same as a beast or summat—and then—"

The man's gesture, brawny fist smashing downward, was eloquent.

Other workmen began to emerge from Troon. They mounted a fleet of bicycles leaning up against the iron railing and made for home and tea. Doctor Dick frowned. Surely the Kinlochs wouldn't—yes. There they were.

"Good afternoon, Doctor Thornton. Oh, I mean Doctor Dick—it's so difficult to bring myself to say that. In town, of course, one's so much more formal. D'you remember Doctor de Tourville, Alice? Imagine if we'd called him Doctor Henry!

Of course he was really a consultant. A very big man. A personal friend of ours."

Doctor Dick let Edith's flow gush right over his head. She'd thought out her speech carefully in order to make two distinct impressions; first as to his regrettable lack of professional dignity, second as to the standing she and Alec had enjoyed in Liverpool. She saw him turn to Lynneth. His rising color she attributed to having got home with her two little stabs. It was always inconceivable to Edith that anyone could just ignore her. She gave them credit for ordinary intelligence.

"You're not—not going over the house so late?"

Doctor Dick had eyes and ears for Lynneth only. Alec, on his way to the front door, turned back and surveyed the doctor with a dull eye of one whose liver is perpetually ill-treated.

"So late!" he echoed. "Late for what? Was old Werne expecting us earlier?"

*

He burst into a high-pitched laugh, disconcerting in a man of his size. Doctor Dick's glance went to the windows of the house before which they stood. He thought he heard a louder, gruffer laugh within—a workman, perhaps. Yes, something dark passed one of the bedroom windows at that moment.

Edith ran forward to the front door, all girlish abandon to take up her husband's witty remark. She lifted the knocker and gave a smart rat-tat-tat.

"We'll ask him if he'll give us tea."

She cast a glassy brown look over the shoulder of her pony-skin coat. Alec, fumbling for his key, laughed again, louder and longer. Edith gave vent to a selection of well-rehearsed "outbursts of merriment." Doctor Dick, alert and listening with painful intentness now, was convinced he heard a hoarse, coarse echo within the walls of Troon. It must be a workman—and—yet—. As he stood there, wondering how on earth he was going to prevent Lynneth from following the two Kinlochs inside, a further shock assaulted his nerves. Alec was still clumsily rooting for his mislaid key.

The heavy front door swung silently, widely open without a touch.

Edith blinked, frowned, assumed a bright tone of playfulness.

"We are invited for tea!" she laughed. "I suppose the men didn't pull the door to. How careless! I shall report it tomorrow' to the foreman. These country yokels! Oh, well, one must be patient, I suppose."

Alec followed his wife inside. Doctor Dick drew Lynneth back.

"Look here—no right to interfere with you and all that—but don't go in!"

Her eyes were fathomless, shining. In the golden dusk her vivid eager face had a transparent look, as if it were wrought glass, golden-tinted, exquisite, through which rare wine sparkled and bubbled and gleamed.

"I—but why do you ask that?"

"Because it's dangerous. It's deadly. Your cousins don't or won't believe anything against Troon. But I tell you the truth. The place is haunted. There's a devil in it."

She looked at him very straightly under the fine beautiful arch of her brows. She knew truth when she heard it. She trusted this man. More than trusted—much, much more than that. For a moment her whole heart responded. Her hands were gripped in his.

"Lynneth! Oh, my dear!" he breathed.

"But—but—" she stammered in surprise. "Is it like this—like this? To feel so sure, when only yesterday—"

The front door banged violently. For a second their startled eyes questioned each other. Then they rushed forward. They had no key. Doctor Dick plied the knocker. Lynneth ran back to the front of the house to peer through the long windows. She returned to Doctor Dick.

"It's all right. Alec's there. He's talking to Edith from the hall. She must be upstairs."

They looked together. Yes, Alec was there safe and sound. He seemed annoyed. Under the hanging unshaded light his face was unhealthily sallow and fretful. His head was flung back.

He was talking to someone above, but no sound was audible to the watchers.

They felt a queer chill of apprehension. His side of the conversation seemed acrimonious, to judge by his expression. His frown became a sullen scowl. He turned from the stairway up which he'd been looking, jammed his hat down, stalked away. Next moment he came outside, leaving the front door open behind him.

"Too damned cold in there to hang about. Edith's as obstinate as—"

He scowled at them, pulled out a pipe, clamped strong yellow teeth on its stem, and began to fill the bowl. After a few puffs he relaxed. Recent and surprising discomfort urged him to speech.

"Chill on my liver or something," he vouchsafed. "Edith insisted—well, you know what she is!" He turned to the girl. "Today's plans included a visitation here," he jerked a thumb inelegantly. "No consideration for my health—must go over the place. Doesn't matter that the house reeks of gas or something. And colder than a tomb. Damn it all, if she must see it, she'll see it without my company!"

Lynneth stared. Never, no, never had she heard him come so near a criticism of his wife. Even when absent in the flesh, her mind ruled his, subjugated it to her opinions. He must be extraordinarily upset.

*

InsideTroon's heavy old walls, Edith went confidently to and fro, snapping on lights, snapping off lights, rubbing a finger on surfaces of wood, raising an eyebrow at a pile of tools and shavings in the middle of a bathroom floor, opening every door in order that air should circulate. The house seemed strangely stuffy, although windows and ventilators were all opened this mild day to dry up paint and varnish and new plaster. And how much colder it was indoors than out! A great golden sun flung a path of light across five miles of sea and sand. Its clear shining reached Troon's gray western face. Six tall west windows met the golden light—and repelled it.

"But how absurd!"

Edith stared about with indignation. Her high heels clicked smartly on woodblock floors as she tried another room. Her room, the room she meant to call her boudoir. The most perfectly preserved in the whole lovely house with its south and west windows, its beams, its old, old corner fireplace so laboriously restored.

"What have they been doing —idiots!" The toffee-brown eyes took on a glaze of anger. "I told them vita-glass in this room. Do they think they can fob off this gray clouded stuff on me? I'd make them come back and change it right away if I were in charge. I shall ring up the contractor tonight. The very idea! These country bumpkins—tiresome things!"

The windows darkened and darkened as she glared about her. So angry was she that a voice from the doorway behind did not startle her at all; it merely represented a person on whom she could vent her vicious mood.

At sight of the big hulking weather-beaten figure in stained ragged jersey and sea-boots, she let fly:

"You're not a workmann here?"

The grizzled ugly head made gesture of denial.

"I'm Mrs. Kinloch."

The man stared, unenlightened by the great news. He was like some great dark bull with his lowered head and bloodshot savage eyes. Edith caught sight of the trail of leaf-mold, mud and dust that marked the intruder's path across polished flooring beyond the doorway.

"Look at the mess you've made. How dare you come tramping about here? Who are you?"

"Thomas Werne."

"Werne! Werne! Why, that's the same name as some unpleasant old man who's supposed to have lived here centuries ago! The one there's such a silly fuss about."

The man appeared uninterested.

"Well! You can go away—at once! D'you hear? Don't imagine because you've the same name as that creature that you've a right of entry to these premises. Be off at once."

He regarded her with a fixed glare. Abruptly he burst into a loud long hoarse laugh. It echoed and re-echoed through the hollow rooms.

Edith drew up her thin person in disgust.

"Really!" She soliloquized without troubling to lower her voice. "Must be a half-wit. These fisherman are the limit. Unpleasant dirty animals. Phew! How dark it's getting. I wish I hadn't stayed after all."

Her glance took in the blank windows, frowned at them. It was almost like an eclipse of the sun, something so queer and sudden and unnatural was in the gloom that spread . . . and spread.

She looked beyond the burly figure in the doorway. An immense skylight was set in the roof above the staircase. When she'd come up only ten minutes ago, clear strong light had shone down. She remembered thinking how well the oak-grain of the steep old stairs showed up after treatment. Now, a wall of impenetrable darkness lay behind the intruder.

Secret inadmissible fear lent a barb to her tongue. Baffled, furious, uncertain, she tried to assume the glacial manner of an aristocrat as she conceived one.

"I don't wish to get you into trouble, my good man, but unless you go—at once—I shall feel it my duty to report you to the police."

A noisy bellow answered her. "Report old Tom Werne, eh! Thot's a good 'un—a reet down dom good 'un!"

His great bulk shook like a jelly. Walls and floor and windows—the whole structure of old Troon seemed to strain and shake and quiver with its uncontrollable amusement.

She stamped her high-heeled shoe, so neat and polished.

"Oh, how dare you! Impertinent—I shall send Mr. Kinloch back to speak to you."

She took a few steps in the gray gloom toward the darker gloom outside, and stopped short. Raging inwardly, she was forced to realize that she couldn't, she positively couldn't make up her mind to go nearer that unpleasant filthy chuckling old beast in the doorway. Should she throw up a window and call to Alec? It would put her in a perfectly idiotic light. Infuriating impasse! She hesitated, summoned her reserves.

"I shall certainly give you in charge," she began. "The moment I—I—"

She blinked, stuttered. Was she mad, or blind, or ill?

Through the windows, golden sun streamed in across the floor, long gleaming ladders of light upon the beautiful wood. The landing outside shone in a yellow haze of cross-lights from open doors on every side. The doorway was empty before her. Empty! The flooring beyond was bare of every trace of dust or leaves.

She stood shivering, spellbound in the quiet sunset glow. Downstairs a door banged like a gun going off. Heavy feet resounded on the red-brick yard at the side of the house. They echoed, died away, swallowed up in the green shadowy depths of the long garden beyond.

*

Released from a spell, she ran downstairs, out the front door, and pulled it after her with an angry bang. She poured out to the waiting three her recent experience. Gesture and phrasing harked back to pre- Lady Bountiful days. Doctor Dick recognized hysteria. Lynneth recognized that sub-Edith she'd always felt but never heard before. Alec did not recognize anything. He regarded her with mulish lack-luster eye.

"You would go over the house! You are so damned obstinate! Must have been old Werne himself you were up there chatting to."

Edith's laugh rose shrill in the cool winter dusk.

"I can believe the doctor might say a thing like that. But you, Alec! Really! What are we coming to!"

"That's what I think. Old Werne himself. I've changed my mind since I went in just now. Not been in such a funk since I was a kid."

"So you left me to face it!"

"I did not. You did all the leaving part. Skipped up the stairs and left me cold. And cold's the word, too. I told you not to go. I knew something beastly was prowling around. Damn it all, you've got nerves of chromium-plated steel."

"Alec! How can you be so silly and so vulgar! Actually using language—in the public street—and to your own wife!"

The shock of it pulled her together quite effectually. She shot across the wide road and began to canter homeward. Alec turned to the doctor and grinned, a shamefaced but quite a human friendly grin.

"See you again, my boy. Looks as if you'd be needed at Troon to give us all nerve tonics and soothing-powders. Well—so long!"

He looked down at Lynneth. One of his more perceptive moments dawned.

"Better get a spot of walk after that scene, my child. I'll toddle home and see to Edith."

He lumbered off, a burly blot of all-British respectability against a sheet of silver water. Doctor Dick turned, eager, ready to make the most of every precious moment. The girl was standing with flower-like face entranced, lips parted, her whole attention absorbed.

"Lynneth! Lynneth darling! What are you looking at inside that horrible old house?"

She did not reply, did not seem to hear. She stood as in a dream, her hands gripping the pointed arrowheads that tipped the iron railing.

"What on earth—?"

He went to her side and peered in through dark blank panes of glass to Troon's lower floor. Darkness. Shadowy darkness.

Chill touched the leaping flame of joy in his heart. He put a hand on hers. She did not move.

"Lynneth! Lynneth!"

The shining of a street lamp showed her face clearly. It was smiling in happy wonder. She seemed intent on some marvel, some vision beyond the big blank windowpanes.

He hesitated. Short of force he couldn't wrench away those small hands that clutched the iron railing. He put an arm about her shoulders, tried to draw her to him, but she did not yield an inch. Her slim soft body might have been one of the iron uprights of the railing. Her eyes didn't flicker from their rapt gaze.

He made up his mind, put out his arms to exert full force, to drag her from Troon, from whatever she saw inside its haunted wall. Abruptly she sighed, loosed her grip, her eyes faded to disappointment, to sick misery.

"Oh, it's gone! The lovely, lovely thing! I can't tell you how lovely. But it's gone. It won't come back. Not now. But I'll watch for it again. I must see it soon again."

The man froze. His blood turned to ice. What deadly perilous thing had she seen? A trap—a snare had been set. For Lynneth—for Lynneth! Oh, God!

To all his anguished questioning she shook her head. Her eyes were sad, full of longing. Remote, distraught, she walked beside him.

"There are no words for it. I can't tell, even if I would. Clouds . . . clouds . . . and a new lovely world. I must go back there—go back—"

He shivered. A devil's trick. Old Werne had played a devil's trick to get her fast. She'd been afraid before. She would have been on guard. Now she only longed to be inside that cursed place, dreamed of it as a wanderer dreams of home.

Their precious hour together was a grim ordeal to him. She, withdrawn and silent, he sick with fear for her. And the end of the nightmare walk was as strange as any of it.

At the black and white gate of Sandilands the two took formal farewell. A rising moon lighted the dark road. On one side of it crouched the little bungalow, looking like a child's toy with its gables, and its fir-trees on either side of the straight formal garden-path. Opposite the odd little dwelling stretched a long meadow. Beyond lay half-drowned marshes—beyond them sand and shining pools left by the tide where seabirds clamored in the moonlight.

Doctor Dick strode away from the gate. He hadn't dreamed such black despair was possible. A voice called him.

"Dick! Dick! I want you. Come back!"

Next moment he had her in his arms. So close, so safe against his heart, it seemed nothing could hurt her again. She put him away at last, laughing, tears gleaming in her eyes.

"What happened to you— darling—darling?" she whispered. "I feel as if I'd waked from a nightmare. Kiss me! Again! Oh, Dick, you do care after all!"

II

"There now, Doctor Dick! Sit down and make yourself at home. It's a week since you've been in. What's worrying you, sir? Tom—a glass of sherry for the doctor."

The host, in blue striped shirtsleeves, apron girt about his beaver waistcoat, clattered off across the red-tiled room. Mrs. Burden looked with keen old eyes at her guest's shadowed face.

"Nothing wrong, so far?"

"No."

His monosyllable dropped like a stone into a deep well. "Nothing. And it's unbearable. The suspense. Waiting—waiting—"

He sprang up, paced to and fro in the leaping firelight, stopped before the quiet watchful old woman, his hands clasped behind his back, legs astride, head thrust forward. She met his searching look and answered his agonized unspoken question in her unhurried fashion.

"Aye. There is danger for the lass every hour she's there. But there's just a gleam of hope to my mind, too."

"For Lynneth! You think so? Why, Mary?"

"That great dark Thing at Troon seems as if it settles on one at a time."

He frowned, stared.

"Then, if so—if so it's Mrs. Kinloch who's in the line of fire. I told you that she saw him—old Werne—and insists he was a drunken fisherman."

Old Mary was emphatic. "It was him. He came with the darkness that's part of him."

"Yes. Mrs. Kinloch admitted the darkness—at first. Went back on it later, though. Said she'd only imagined it got dark."

"She saw Werne. It's my belief she'll go next. Then you can take your lass away."

"But, good heavens! D'you mean I'm to wait until that devil murders Mrs. Kinloch?"

"What other way is there?" Her calm matter-of-factness roused in him a sudden hysterical desire to roar with laughter. And after all, he had to wait! If that obstinate woman—

"I've asked her a dozen times to leave Troon. She's on the point of forbidding me the house," he admitted.

"Waste no more words," advised the old woman. "They'll take you nowhere. Your job is to save the lass. Never mind fretting over them as are blind and deaf as stones."

Old Tom returned and poured the wine. Doctor Dick sat down, glass in hand.

"How about the servant lassies at Troon?" asked Mr. Burden.

"From Liverpool," the doctor said. "They've heard nothing so far, Dressed up town girls, too superior to be friendly with Seagate fishermen. They've only one complaint so far."

"Aye!"

"They say Troon's dark. Grumble about the windows— that the glass is always gray and clouded even when the sun's shining outside."

"Darkness. 'Thing of Darkness'—that's what parson called it the day he buried Joe Dawlish."

"Thing of Darkness." Doctor Dick rose. His face was drawn and stern. "Well, I must be off. I'm dining at Troon. A housewarming. I'll call in again after it's over. It's likely to be a housewarming that leaves me cold." The heavy door clanged behind him.

"He'll not come back this night." Mrs. Burden turned a solemn face to her husband. He sat in his favorite chair, drawing on his churchwarden. "Friday, 'tis! And full moon.

And—I didn't tell Doctor Dick purposely—he's enough on his mind— but it's the anniversary of the day Lizzie Werne disappeared. It's written in that old book I told you of. December 2nd, 1636."

"You think old Werne'll—?"

"Aye. I think he will."

*

"You must excuse this picnic meal." Edith's eyes were ablaze with triumph. Hard bright color dyed her thin cheeks. "I warned you it would be a case of roughing it. The maids have done their best, but you know what they are!"

Four sat at the gate-legged table of Jacobean oak for dinner that night, the seventh night of the Kinloch's arrival at Troon. Edith had worked like a beaver, had driven cook and housemaid before her whirl of energy like galley-slaves. The big gaunt house was furnished from wide shadowy attics to scrubbed and scoured kitchens and pantries.

Doctor Dick remembered the Biblical story of the man possessed of a devil, who swept and garnished his house. He remembered and shivered.

He made the reply his hostess expected of him. The well-pointed table, the gleaming silver and dinner service chosen to harmonize with the house, the five-course dinner, the well-trained maids imported from town, were all elaborate and over-emphatic in perfection. Not the natural and dignified background of a well-bred hostess, but a show. Herself the blatant complacent showman!

"Alone I did it," her voice, manner, and conversation implied.

"You know," she reproached the visitor, "I really believe you're disappointed. I think I see—yes, I'm sure I do—a sort of I'd rather that my friend should die than my prediction prove a lie expression on your face."

Alec intervened. He, at least, had the advantage of early discipline that had planted certain fixed rules of conduct in him. Doctor Dick looked ill at ease. He must be soothed. Hang it all, you didn't rub things in at your own dinner-table! Edith was a bit above herself tonight. She'd got her way. They were living at Troon. Things were all right too—at least—He brushed away suspicion. Just an effect of lighting. He wasn't used to the queer old house yet.

"Noticed the fireplace?" he asked. "It's part of the original tavern. Sort of bakehouse. The whole inglenook, arches and chimney breast and the little iron door to shove ashes through, were covered up by a kitchen-range. Lovely old stuff that brick —three hundred years old."

Thankfully, the guest accepted the diversion.

"Makes a wonderful dining room. That window too, I like the square panes—different from the silly imitations they make. Set in that battered old framework it's—hello! Who's that looking in? D'you keep a gardener working at this hour?"

Edith glanced up quickly, wished she'd drawn the curtains after all. She'd decided, on such a romantic moonlight night, that the vista of garden enhanced the room's perfection. Impatiently she tinkled a small copper bell at her hand. No one answered it. She rang again, waited. No sound from outside.

Lynneth ventured a suggestion. She was in one of the strange dreamy moods that the doctor dreaded—moods that had recurred again and again since that night of her "vision," as she called it. Her dinner-gown of smoke-gray velvet with its gleam of gold thread, the jewel—Tiger's Tear—glinting tawny-yellow on her breast, the thick shining hair like folded wings about her head, all gave Doctor Dick a pang of terror and dismay. She looked unreal tonight, held in dreams, unaware of evil, of danger coming stealthily nearer as she slept.

"I think," the girl's voice was only a whisper, "I think they've gone away. Someone—came for them."

Edith's answer was sharp with vexation. "My dear girl, what an idea! Go away in the middle of my dinner party? Why? They don't know a soul here. Really, Lynneth! You look half asleep. You'd better go and look for them. It might rouse you."

Doctor Dick sprang to his feet. "No. Let me go, please!"

Edith raised resigned exasperated brows. He would behave like this. How irritating these unconventional people were! He seemed to think this was a picnic, after all. Taken her literally. So stupid! Spoiling the whole tone of her dinner. Now they'd all have to get up. She and Alec couldn't sit still and let a guest chase about the house.

She rose, stood with finger-tips on the table, lifted her chin, looked around from under lowered lids in what she knew to be a really compelling pose. Her Queen Elizabeth look, she termed it privately. More privately still, she was sure there was some strain of royal blood in her. Some ancestor of hers had been—er—naughty! Oh, she was sure. How else did she come by the profound conviction of her own superiority? She knew she was different—an aristocrat deep down.

"I will go myself," she pronounced. "I insist. The maids are my province, after all."

Lynneth was unmoved by majesty's withdrawal. She seemed to be listening to some far-off entrancing sound. The two men looked uncertainly at each other. Alec assumed a boisterous hearty manner.

"Drink up, drink up! Fill your glass, my boy, and pass the claret along. The girls are new to Seagate. Heard something and dashed out to investigate, I expect. You know how pin-headed they are."

Minutes passed. No sound from hall or kitchens. Then came the tap-tap of high heels just overhead.

"Edith! Girls must've gone upstairs, not outside. I wonder—"

"We ought to go up, too."

Doctor Dick was on his feet. Alec, puzzled and uncomfortably disturbed by something he did not begin to understand, rose also. They made for the door. The doctor turned back, to see Lynneth sitting peacefully at the table, dreaming, indifferent.

"Stay there. Don't move from this room," he called back. "Lynneth! Lynneth!"

She responded with a vague absent smile. Doctor Dick followed his host with a last anxious look of love at the girl. A sense of mortal deadly peril threatened. The whole house seemed growing dark and suffocating and evil.

A cry came from above. Every light dimmed, went out. Thick choking darkness muffled Troon from kitchens to attics. Blindly, Doctor Dick fought his way up.

"Where are you?" he called.

From the stairs above, he heard Alec's voice, muffled, cursing.

"What's wrong? What are you doing? Can't you answer me, man?"

"I'm trying—to—get down." Alec's voice came thicker, fainter now. A stumble. Curses and sound of hoarse hurried breathing in the darkness above. Then there was a yell—the crack of splintering wood—a heavy body came slithering and sprawling down the stairs as if flung with immense force. It knocked against Doctor Dick as he was stumbling upward, and he fell too, slipping down until an angle in the wall stopped him. Winded, uninjured, uncertain what to do next, he called out.

"Lynneth! Lynneth! Are you all right? Can you find matches? I left my lighter in my overcoat." No answer from the profound darkness below.

"Lynneth!"

A voice, a vague faint echo of the girl's clear tone, floated down from above, it seemed to him. He made his way up the steep narrow old stairs again. "Lynneth! Lynneth!"

Edith Kinloch, cinnamon-brown silk flounces rustling her indignation, pursued her search. The kitchens, the pantries, were ablaze with light. And the hall. And the landing upstairs. She looked quickly into the rooms on the ground floor. No one there. But every room was brilliantly lighted.

She stamped her annoyance. Was this some low silly joke? Had the two maids gone off for some reason, leaving on all the lights merely to upset her? But why? Why? There had been no trouble over anything. Later perhaps, when they knew she did not intend to get more help—

She ran upstairs. Here again all lights were on. Every bedroom door was flung widely open. The blood rose to her head. In a rage now, she went up the last steep twisting staircase to the attics, and once more found the same silly prank had been played. True the lights were less brilliant. Fifteens were good enough for maids to waste! They'd only read in bed and be late in the morning if she gave them stronger lamps.

She hadn't thought fifteens were quite so poor though. Why, one candle would give more light than these things. Must be faulty bulbs. She'd ring up and complain tomorrow. They seemed to be getting dimmer as she looked at them. One died right out overhead. The one over the stairwell. She'd turn her ankle getting down again.

But where were those fools of girls? She stalked across to the wardrobe. There hung the tweed coats they wore, and a lot of other clothes. They couldn't have run off. They must be in the garden. She'd go down and send Alec out to find them.

Lynneth would have to make coffee and serve it, to cover the gap. Thank heaven, they'd finished the last course, anyhow. She turned about on the square landing, a mere three-foot platform, from which the attics opened.

In the big west room a sound brought her head about with a jerk.

"Who's there? Is that you, Beasley? Parkes?"

A shuffle. A heavy tread. She went back to the room. A light clicked off in the room as she entered it. She wheeled with a little squeal of anger.

"How dare you—"

*

In the darkness, a blacker deadlier darkness moved. Held rigid in sudden cold fear, her eyes accustomed themselves to the gloom. The window stood widely open. No. Not open. She looked at the thing. No window or even frame was there. Merely a ruinous irregular break in the crumbling wall.

She went to it, dizzy, sick, her nostrils filled with dusty choking stench. Her eyes followed the swelling shapeless Thing of Darkness that moved in the moonlit darkness of the room. A sudden red light shone from a foul little lantern that stood on a stone shelf formed by the chimney-breast's irregularities. Bare crumbling brick, the chimney was.

"But this"—she spoke aloud in a hoarse amazed voice—"this is what it was before we restored it. This isn't our Troon!"

"No. It's mine."

Loud voice and louder laughter answered her. She recognized them. In the smoking lamplight, she saw the vast ugly bulk, the bloated face, the small cruel eyes set under matted hair.

"You! You here again! I thought I told you—"

Her voice died. Her cold hands flew to her throat. She pressed back—back against the dirty old wall behind. The other attic was darkened now; her frightened eyes glanced across to it. She was up here in the dark, shut up with this brutal mad old man. It was a trick! Those servants! She'd have them punished. A monstrous experience! How dare they let her be subjected to it!

Ah!—he was moving nearer—nearer—darkness, thick black choking darkness, rolled forward like a tidal wave.

Now it touched her. She shrieked. Ice-cold, wet, like rotting slime, it touched her—closer about her—closer! Backward she went before the stifling death-back to the gaping ruinous wall. If she could get to that—call for help! Yes! Yes! She was on her knees on the dusty uneven broken flooring. With desperate effort she twisted, thrust her head outside.

"Help! Help!" she shrieked. "Help!"

The word choked in her throat. She was drawn back, as if the room were a quicksand into which she sank—down—down—silken flounces ripped— hair fallen all about her face of idiot terror—down—down—through the door of life—down through hell's dark gates—down—down—the Thing of Darkness pressed closer—-closer still. . . .

*

It seemed to Doctor Dick, fighting his way in the unnatural darkness, as if he struggled up through clouds of poisonous gas whose fumes took strength from his limbs, sight from his eyes. Gasping. Dragging himself up one stair at a time. A cold numbness invaded him.

Then a frightful bubbling shriek pierced his senses. It came from above. Another—and more horrible cry. He groaned. He couldn't hurry. He felt consciousness being blotted out. Darkness pressed on him like solid walls. A stench of rotted decay filled his nostrils, choked the breath in his throat . . . it failed him . . . he fell forward.

Darkness flowed over him like the river of death itself.

He opened his eyes to find himself lying on the stairs just below the first-floor landing. Electric lights winked on all sides. Gray dawn met his aching bewildered eyes through a vast skylight overhead.

He tried to think, to remember as he struggled to rise. How had he come there? Why did such heavy desperate weariness weigh him down?

Sick, trembling with effort, he stood clinging to the baluster-rail. Below, under the glare of a droplight, he caught sight of a man sprawled untidily across a glowing Persian rug. Groaning, he stumbled down to investigate.

It was Alec who lay there. Doctor Dick's professional instinct pricked him from lethargy as he examined the man. "Broken leg, slight concussion." he murmured. Suddenly full recollection flashed in his clouded mind.

"Lynneth! Lynneth!" he called aloud.

He made for the dining-room where he had left her last night. The place was deserted. Lights gleamed dismally in the half daylight. The dinner-table's bravery of silver and glass mocked his distraught gaze. He searched the lower rooms. No one.

He passed Alec as if he'd been part of the hall furniture, and went upstairs. Lights burned everywhere. The air was chill but clean. Empty room after empty room greeted him vacantly. Only the last narrow stairs now to the wide attics above.

"Lynneth!"

He sprang up the topmost flight, and crouched beside the crumpled heap of gray velvet.

*

Her dark head was against the wall, blood stained her face, her soft white neck, the bosom of her dress. The Tiger's Tear had fallen back against her parted lips—gleaming golden bauble.

Wild meaningless phrases shot into his distraught mind. Bits of Ecclesiastes: "The silver cord is loosed . . . the golden bowl—"

He touched her, bent closer. Ah, it was not death after all! Not death. He was all physician now. The healer. Dare he lift her to examine further? That head wound was very deep—blood still welling. His eyes grew cold with fear once more as he explored it. The skull was crushed at one place. How could he move her from that awkward corner? It would be fatal to jolt her wounded head.

He hesitated only a moment. He must do it, of course. He daren't leave her alone in Troon while he got help. And every second counted. If ever he thanked heaven for his strength, it was now. When, with infinite care, he'd laid her down at last on a bed in the nearest room on the floor below the attics, he went to the bathroom.

From an elaborately fitted-out medicine chest there, on which Edith had greatly plumed herself, he dug out what he could. Gray dawn brightened today as he fought to save Lynneth. He used what makeshift medicaments he had. Dark hair he'd cut away was strewn on a pale costly rug beside the bed. The girl's face looked carved from frozen snow beneath its bandages. Her pulse beat ominously slow beneath his touch.

Her life hung balanced by a thread, and he watched with increasing fear. She must lie undisturbed now for another twenty-four hours at least. There was a slim, a very slim chance of life—no chance at all if she moved.

*

But there was another night to face—another night at Troon. How could he protect her? What weapons could a man use against the Thing of Darkness? Brooding, pondering, dazed with the terrific strain of the past hours, he sat. A creaking sound startled him.

It was Mrs. Burden. She was coming upstairs. He took her hands, kissed her withered cheek, tears of relief in his eyes at sight of the old woman's calm face and faithful eyes.

"You're a miracle. No one in the world but you would have come. Now perhaps—"

He poured out in brief hurried whispers what he'd seen and heard last night.

"Servants gone. Kinloch's smashed up. Edith Kinloch's gone. I couldn't look for her. I daren't leave Lynneth alone for a minute in this house."

"Best look now, sir. I'll bide with your lass."

She settled down beside the patient like a little brown bird, watching the unconscious girl, taking in the room with clear thoughtful old eyes.

Doctor Dick went upstairs to begin his search. She heard him coming slowly down at last; heard his heavy breathing as if he carried some awkward weight. He had to pass the open door of the room where she sat. She saw what it was he carried.

Its broken neck revealed what once had been a human face— now a darkened dreadful mask. A few tattered wisps of silk clung to the broken body. Jeweled rings glittered on limp and dusty hands.

Doctor Dick passed on, went into a room nearby. When he came in to her again he looked like an old man.

"You saw—it?"

Mrs. Burden nodded solemnly. "Wait here, sir. Coffee laced with brandy is what you need. We'll talk when you're better, my lamb—sir, I mean—begging your pardon!"

"Wait!" His hoarse voice detained her. "There's Kinloch, poor chap! Must see to him. Help me lift him. I don't think he's seriously hurt."

"There's no way out. We've got to spend this coming night at Troon. The chances are we'll go" —Doctor Dick made a gesture to the bedroom across the landing— "like . . . that!"

"No. Not like that. Whatever comes, not like that. It's true, as you said, 'tis no good letting any other body come inside this place. 'Tis for you and me—this night's work. No one else can help. Even the vicar himself couldn't. 'Tis for you and me. But no one of us will go—the way she did! No. If we have to die, I can take the three of us an easier road than that."

Day faded. Its last gold shone above the distant hills. A gleaming path lay across the water. The gold dimned, and died. Darkness began to fall. Shadows thickened within the walls of Troon.

Mrs. Burden got up from her chair, beckoned the doctor to the door of Lynneth's room.

"You must leave things to me from this hour on. Keep your door fast bolted inside. Don't open it, not even if you think you hear my own voice call. 'Twould be a trick of old Werne that—to get you out of here. For God's sake, Doctor Dick, heed what I'm telling you. Stay inside until daylight comes. Bide with your lass here, if you want her to live, and want to live yourself."

"If you'd only tell me what you're up to, Mary! It's horrible to shut you out, to leave you alone—with that devilish thing."

"Eh, haven't we talked enough o' that? All the day long you've argued wi' me, Doctor Dick, and I tell you mind's made up. I'm old, too old to fear death. And I know things—things I can't tell you, sir. Bolt the door—and leave it fast till daylight."

*

Moving with sure unhurried purpose outside the bolted door, Mrs. Burden went to and fro among the shifting looming shadows. She had all prepared. She made no mistake.

There was only one way to shut out a damned soul. The cross itself. A cross of living flesh and blood.

In the wood-frame of the door, outside, four great hooks had been screwed in by Doctor Dick that day. Iron hooks that Mrs. Burden had brought prepared for her purpose, two at the top corners of the cross-piece, and one on either side of the door.

From these hooks she hung four plaited loops of hair and hempen rope—two long loops from the top, two very short ones on either side.

She stood with back against door and slipped the long right-hand loop beneath her left arm pit, and the long left-hand loop beneath her right armpit. Then, supported so that fatigue should not make her fall, she thrust her hands through the small handcuff loops on either side to keep her arms straight out from her body.

So she stood, a small light bird-like figure. Through the big-roof-window, glimmering stars and rising moon showed her in the dusk, a human crucifix past which the Thing of Darkness might not go.

Facing Troon and its evil. Frail old body. Staunch old soul.

*

Daylight. Daylight and Lynneth had passed the crisis! She was safe. Doctor Dick opened the door. The light worn body of Old Mary hung there still.

It was an empty shrine, too old, too tired to survive the night's long vigil and shock of battle—an empty shrine, but not marred, not touched by hurt or evil. The Thing Of Darkness had left no shadow in the calm sightless eyes, no lines of terror or dismay on the peaceful worn old face; only deep exhaustion. A victor fallen at the goal.

A victor. Yes, Doctor Dick knew that. For long minutes he looked at the frail triumphant figure, assurance of her victory deep in his heart; giving homage to the dead, giving thanks for her divine courage.

His eyes, blinded with tears, lifted to see something else at last, A hulking black-haired man stood against an opposite wall. As the doctor stared, red sunrise dyed the skylight window above, touched the ugly brutal figure with flame.

It shrank, quivered. Its purple lips opened in soundless rage. Its dark bulk glowed like molten metal. White-hot . . . sullen red . . . dissolving . . . writhing . . . twisting in the sun's merciless fire to inhuman appalling decay—to a rag and wisp of a thing—to a shriveled black mummy that grinned in age-old death.

That too dissolved and was split like sand running through an hourglass. It lay on the jade-green Chinese carpet, a drift of gray dust, last grim symbol of mortality.

The shadow-life that Werne had bargained for was finished. Soul, will, poisonous hate were blotted out. The blackest magic could perpetuate his borrowed existence no longer. The deepest hell could offer no shelter for his furious ghost. Werne—Thing of Darkness—was no more.

But the old house still fronts sea and sky hills. Troon—old Troon. Shell of death. Desolate. Betrayed.

Lightning Source UK Ltd.
Milton Keynes UK
UKOW051950180613

212473UK00002B/163/P